Don't
Call Me
Beanhead!

Don't Call Me Beanhead!

Susan Wojciechowski

illustrated by
Susanna Natti

CANDLEWICK PRESS
CAMBRIDGE, MASSACHUSETTS

★

With love, for my sister Jean
who helped make it all happen

First published by Candlewick Press

CANDLEWICK PRESS
2067 MASSACHUSETTS AVENUE
CAMBRIDGE MA 02140

Thanks to Susanna Natti's daughter, Kate Willsky,
for her advice on Beany's drawings.

ISBN 0-590-13924-X

12 11 10   9/9 0 1 2/0

Printed in the U.S.A.   40

First Scholastic printing, May 1997

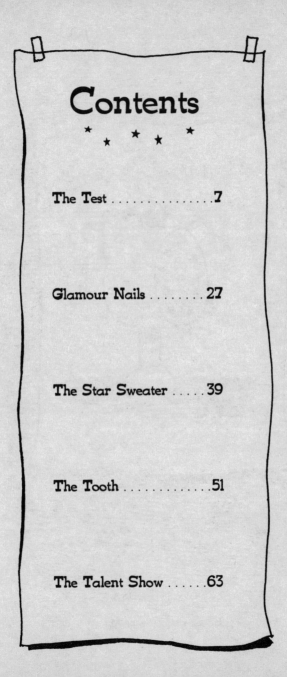

Contents

★ ★ ★ ★ ★

The Test

* * * *

My teacher, Ms. Babbitt, wears a different pair of earrings practically every day of the year. She has heart earrings for Valentine's Day, pumpkins for Halloween, turkeys for Thanksgiving, candy canes for Christmas. She has snowmen, flowers, leaves, and American flags. She has big, dangly smiley faces for days when something fun is going to happen and question marks for days when she's going to give a test.

One day she walked into the classroom after lunch wearing the question marks. All of us except Catherine Pruitt, the class brain, groaned. Ms. Babbitt went to the blackboard and wrote:

Science Quiz—Healthy Bodies:

1. Name two things that are harmful to health and tell their bad effect on the body.
2. Name one food at the bottom of the food pyramid and one food at the top.
3. Name four ways to keep our bodies healthy.

I took a sheet of paper out and wrote: **Bernice Sherwin-Hendricks**. That's my name. I'm named Bernice after my great grandma. And I'm Sherwin-Hendricks on account of my mother sticking her last name onto my dad's when they got married, which I hate because it takes so long to write. I would like to write just plain Beany on my papers, but my teacher does not allow nicknames. So on paper I am Bernice Sherwin-Hendricks, but in talking I am Beany. Except if you're mad at me. Then you could call me Bernice Lorraine Sherwin-Hendricks, which is what my mother calls me when she's mad. Do not call me Beanhead, though. Ever. My big brother Philip calls me that, and I hate it.

After my name I put: **Science**. Then I put my teacher's name, **Ms**. **Babbitt**. I like her. She smells nice. After that I put the date. All that stuff together is called the heading, which is what we have to put on every single paper even if it is just a spelling pretest.

After the heading I skipped a line and put:

1. Smoking can give you lung cancer.
   Taking bad drugs can fry your brain.

2. Spaghetti is at the bottom of the food pyramid.
   Candy and junk food are at the top.

I was just writing a number 3 on my paper when, out of the corner of my eye, I saw something moving. It was an ant carrying a big crumb of food along the top of the bookcase next to my desk. I watched the ant go around a box of rulers and over a stack of workbooks. I watched it climb up a plant and walk all over the leaves before it figured out which way was down.

By the time the ant got to the end of the bookcase, I had named it Hulk. I watched Hulk climb up the pencil sharpener and go marching right into one of the pencil holes.

"Come on, Hulk, get out of there," I whispered nervously when the ant didn't come out for a few seconds. Just then, Kevin Gates got up and walked over to the sharpener. I jumped out of my chair so fast that it fell over. I jumped right in front of Kevin.

Most of the time I'm scared of him. Kevin knocks my lucky eraser off my desk when he walks by, and blows milk at people through his straw, and cuts in line in front of people. He even cut ahead of me once when I was line leader, but I was too scared of him

to tell. This time, though, I didn't even think about it. I just told Kevin, "You can't use the sharpener."

Kevin pushed me. "You and what army's gonna stop me, Beany weenie?" he asked, and lifted his pencil toward the hole. Just in time, Hulk came out of the hole and went on his way, lugging the crumb down the side of the bookcase and out of sight, like he didn't have a care in the world, like he hadn't just taken his life in his hands by going into that sharpener, like he hadn't just put me in danger of getting punched on the arm by Kevin after school in the bus line.

I went back to my desk. I picked up my chair. I picked up my pencil and wrote: **Four ways to keep our bodies healthy are** . . .

Before I could write any more, Ms. Babbitt said, "Time is up. Please pass your papers forward."

My face got all hot. It was the first time in my whole life I hadn't finished a test. I knew I would flunk "Healthy Bodies." Just to keep from crying I made myself think of something happy. I thought about the time I went to a horse farm with the Brownie Scouts and rode on a horse named Mr. Bumble and fed him a carrot and he didn't even eat my hand off.

The next Monday, Ms. Babbitt walked up and down the aisles giving back the tests. When she handed me mine I saw a big red F at the top. The first thing I did was crumple up the paper and stick it inside my desk. The second thing I did was blame Hulk for making me flunk. The third thing I did was think about Mr. Bumble, the horse.

"I would like you children to take these quizzes home, have them signed by a parent, and return them tomorrow," Ms.

Babbitt said, as I was closing my desk lid.

I pulled the wrinkled test from under my math book. All afternoon I kept worrying about how I would tell my parents I flunked. It's not that my parents are mean. It's just that I worry about things. Once I had a rash on my thumb and I worried that my thumb would fall off. When I go on the ferris wheel at the amusement park I worry that my car will come unhooked and fall down. I never leave my seat to go buy popcorn at the movies because I worry that I won't be able to find the seat when I come back. My mother calls me a worrywart.

On the bus ride home Carol Ann, who lives two houses from me and is in my class, asked what I got on my test.

"You know Ms. Babbitt doesn't like us to tell other people our grades," I answered.

"You flunked, huh?"

"Yeah." I showed Carol Ann the test.

"It's pretty wrinkled," she said. She smoothed out the paper and read what Ms. Babbitt had put at the top, next to the F: "This is not your best work, Bernice."

"You could be in big trouble," Carol Ann told me. "Your parents might not sign it. Or they might punish you by not letting you watch TV for a year, not even Saturday morning cartoons. They might even ask for a meeting with Ms. Babbitt."

"What am I going to do?"

"Well," said Carol Ann, "you could try what my big sister Margo did once when she flunked a math test and had to get it signed. She put the paper in with a whole stack of other papers and told my dad he had to sign all of them. She figured he would get so tired that pretty soon he'd stop looking at the papers and just sign."

"Did it work?"

"No way. He yelled so loud I thought I'd bust an eardrum, but maybe your dad isn't as smart as my dad."

We got off the bus at our street. Just as I was stuffing the paper into my backpack, a gust of cold March wind came along and snatched it away. For a second I thought all my problems were solved. It would blow away into the clouds.

But then I realized the paper might not blow into the clouds. It might blow over to the laundromat around the corner and someone might pick it up and put it on the bulletin board inside the door. Then the whole neighborhood would think that Bernice Sherwin-Hendricks doesn't even know four ways to keep her body healthy.

Or it might blow two streets down and stop right on Boomer Fenton's front steps. It's not that I like Boomer or anything like that, even though he gave me a valentine this year that had a picture of an ice cube tray on it with one ice cube saying to another, "You're cool," and I gave him a valentine of two monkeys in a tree that said, "I'm ape over you."

Really, I don't like Boomer. I just sit with him on the bus sometimes so I can see the birthmark on his arm that looks like a dog's head.

I decided I wouldn't want my test to land

on his front steps where he might see it and stop thinking I'm cool and stop letting me look at his dog birthmark.

Carol Ann and I ran after the paper. Every time it came to a stop and one of us was about to grab it, the wind would blow it away again. Finally, Carol Ann caught up with it and jumped on it with both feet. I reached down and grabbed at it. I got the paper, but the corner where Carol Ann was standing ripped off.

It looked pretty sad, all wrinkled and torn and covered with dirty sneaker prints. When I got home I showed it to my big brother, Philip, and asked him what he thought Mom and Dad would do when they saw it.

"You're dead, Beanhead," he said, and went back to looking at himself in the mirror. Philip is thirteen and looks in the mirror a lot. I tried it once to see what could be so

much fun about looking in the mirror for half an hour, but all I saw were my fat cheeks—which my brother says look like a chipmunk's cheeks when they're full of nuts—and my twenty-three freckles.

When I thought about Philip saying I was dead and Carol Ann saying I might not get to watch TV for a year, I decided to use Carol Ann's plan. I put three papers on top of my science test. One was a math paper that said, "This is fine work, Bernice." One was a workbook page from last year that the teacher had put a smiley face on. One was a spelling test with 100% written at the top in red.

I waited for just the right time to give the papers to Mom or Dad. But the right time didn't come. At bedtime I finally had to do it, right time or not. Mom was at the kitchen table paying bills and talking to her checkbook, which meant it was a bad time to give them to her. Dad was in front of the TV watching a basketball game and punching the arm of his chair every few seconds, which meant it was a bad time to give them to him.

I decided to leave them with Dad since he was in a dark room. I put the papers on the floor in front of him and told him to sign them whenever he had time. Then I ran up to my room and jumped into bed with my stuffed moose, Jingle Bell. I pulled the covers over our heads and told Jingle Bell the whole story about Hulk and flunking the test and Carol Ann's plan. Jingle Bell understood. He always does.

For a while I could hear Dad yelling, "Come on, Celtics." Then a commercial came on. After a minute I heard Dad coming slowly up the stairs.

I pretended to be asleep. I squeezed my eyes shut tight. My heart was pounding fast. Dad sat down on the edge of my bed.

"Beany," he said, as he pulled the covers off my head, "these are super papers."

I opened my eyes wide. I sat up. It had worked! Carol Ann's dumb idea had worked!

"All except for the bottom one," he went on.

"Daddy, it wasn't my fault," I said, talking as fast as I could. "It was all the dumb ant's fault. Hulk was so dumb he almost got lost

in the pencil sharpener. And it was Kevin's fault, too. He shouldn't have been sharpening a pencil right in the middle of a test. And Ms. Babbitt shouldn't have let him—it's a rule about 'Don't leave your seat during a test.' And Carol Ann—she told me to trick you. It was all her fault. And Philip scared me. He told me I was dead."

Dad put his hand gently over my mouth. "Beany, you seem to be blaming an awful lot of people for this. The only name I haven't heard is yours. Now calm down and tell me what happened."

After I told him the whole story and told him the only reason I tricked him was on account of not wanting to miss Saturday morning cartoons till I'm grown up, he said, "Do you think you're the first kid on earth ever to have a problem in school?"

"Well, I bet you never did," I said.

"Yes, I did. My fifth grade teacher once sent a note home to my mother when I got into a fight at school. I was so scared I hid in my closet for six hours. My parents looked everywhere for me. They thought I was kidnapped."

"But then they found you and hugged you and everything was fine. Right, Dad?"

"Not on your life. I wasn't allowed out of the house to play for a month."

I started to cry. I knew I was in trouble, even more trouble than the time I saw a frog hopping around near the front door of my school and let it in.

"Don't worry, Beany," Dad said. "I signed the paper. I know you do your best in school. But from now on, promise me you'll be honest?"

"I promise."

"And you won't try to trick me, even if Carol Ann thinks it's a good idea?"

"I won't."

"And whose fault was the F?"

"Well, sort of mine."

Daddy kissed me, first on my forehead, then on my nose. I hugged him so hard he grunted. Then he tucked me and Jingle Bell under the covers and wiped my tears with his big bandana handkerchief.

The next morning at the bus stop, Carol Ann asked me how it had gone.

"My dad signed the paper."

"Your problems aren't over, you know," she told me. "You have to explain to Ms. Babbitt why your paper looks like it went through a war."

"I'm dead," I said.

"Want to know what I did when my dog chewed my homework to shreds?"

"No!" I yelled at Carol Ann. I got on the bus and sat next to Boomer Fenton.

Glamour Nails

* * * *

I was in my bedroom pulling out all the stuff from under my bed trying to find a jump rope, when I heard Carol Ann outside yelling, "Beany! Come on out. I have something to show you."

I went outside and Carol Ann started dancing around in front of me me waving her hands in my face. Her nails were long, and they were glittery gold.

"How did your nails grow so fast?" I asked her.

"They didn't, silly. These are Glamour Nails. Don't you know anything?"

Carol Ann is four months older than me and thinks she knows everything. She once told me that if you need to wear glasses it means you're smart. Carol Ann wears glasses. Another time she said she read in a magazine that teachers like students with curly hair better than students with straight hair. Carol Ann's hair looks like yellow spiral macaroni.

She showed me the Glamour Nails package. At the top it said, "Add Excitement to Your Life." At the bottom it said, "Choose from five wild and wonderful colors: Very

Cherry, Purple Passion, Pink Icing, Glimmering Gold, and Sparkling Silver."

I wanted the Sparkling Silver. I wanted to glue them over my nails that are all short and stubby from biting them.

If I had long, Sparkling Silver nails I could wave them in front of Carol Ann's face. I could pretend I was a princess, and everyone in my kingdom would come to watch me wave my sparkling hands gracefully in front of them.

"How much?" I asked Carol Ann.

"Three dollars plus tax at Mayer's Drugstore."

"Mom!" I yelled. "Where are you?"

"I'm in the backyard," she called back. I raced to the backyard where my mother was hanging wash on the clothesline.

"Mom," I said, "if I ask you for something will you say yes?"

"What is it?" Mom said as she shook out a sheet and clipped it to the line.

"This is something I really, really want more than anything in the whole world."

"What is it?" she said again.

"Can I have three dollars plus tax for a set of Glamour Nails? Please, please, pretty please with sugar and gummy bears on top?"

"What on earth are Glamour Nails?" my mom wanted to know.

"They're fake nails. They come in five wild and wonderful colors and will make my life exciting."

"Why don't you think about it for a while and if you still want them a week from now, we'll talk about it then."

"I have been thinking about it and I really want them. If you buy them for me I'll never ask you for anything again, ever, ever."

"Well, if you want Glamour Nails so badly that you can't think it over for one week, you'll have to buy them with your own money, and you may not wear the nails to school, only for play," Mom answered.

Carol Ann and I went up to my room. I pried off the top of my Tootsie Roll bank and poured the money onto my desk. Carol Ann couldn't help me sort the coins because of her nails being too long to pick up any of them. So I put all the coins in piles, then counted. I had a dollar and sixty-three cents.

"You'll need over a dollar more. Two

dollars more would do it for sure," Carol Ann said.

"How will I get two dollars?"

"Could you borrow it from your brother?"

We found Philip in his bedroom looking at himself in the mirror.

"Philip, could you lend me two dollars?" I asked.

"In your dreams, Beanhead," he said. I figured that meant no.

Carol Ann and I went back to my room to think.

"Maybe you could sell something," she suggested.

"What do I have to sell?"

"People like shiny things. Find something shiny," said Carol Ann.

"And glittery. People like glittery things," I added, poking through the pile of stuff I had pulled out from under my bed.

"If you want to sell something for two dollars it should be big," Carol Ann added.

"Yes, big and heavy. Someone would definitely pay two dollars for something that's big and heavy and shiny and glittery."

Then I got an idea. We went to the backyard and dug up one of the big rocks that edge my mom's flower garden. Carol Ann and I carried it in to the sink and washed it clean. Then we smeared white glue all over it and I sprinkled a tube of red glitter onto the rock. Finally we sprayed it with hair spray to make it shine.

It looked awesome.

We showed it to Mikey next door. Mikey is four. Mikey loved the rock. He ran indoors to get two dollar bills out of his bank.

Carol Ann and I rode our bikes to Mayer's Drugstore a block away, where I bought a package of Sparkling Silver Glamour Nails. When we got home I saw Mikey sitting on his front porch steps next to the rock. The rock was not covered with red sparkles. Mikey's hands, face, and shirt were. He was crying and his mom was trying to wipe the tears and the sparkles off his face.

When Carol Ann saw Mikey, she jumped on her bike and took off.

"Chicken!" I yelled after her.

I walked slowly over to Mikey's porch. I told Mrs. Novak the whole story. I told her I was sorry. I said I would pay Mikey back as soon as I returned the nails. I told her I would wash his shirt but she told me that I had done enough already.

The next day when Carol Ann came over to play she was wearing only six of her Glamour Nails. She told me the other four had fallen off during the night and she still hadn't found them. She did not look glamorous. She did not look exciting. How she looked was weird.

"Beany," she said, "wait till you see what I have." Out of her pocket she pulled a ring with a gray stone in it. When she put it on her finger, the stone turned yellow. I tried it on and the stone turned blue.

"Is it a magic ring?" I asked Carol Ann.

"No, silly. Don't you know anything? It's

a mood ring. It changes color depending on your mood. Blue means exciting. Yellow means gentle."

"Wow! Where did you get it?"

"Mayer's Drugstore. Four dollars plus tax."

I ran into the kitchen where Mom was reading the paper.

"Mom," I said, "if I ask you for something will you say yes? The Glamour Nails were dumb. A mood ring is what I really, really, really, *really* want."

The
Star Sweater

* * * *

Last Valentine's Day Ms. Babbitt told us to make a list of the things we love. I think she did it to stall for time till dismissal. We had read all our valentines and pigged out on candy hearts, cupcakes with pink frosting, and cherry Kool-Aid. Some of the boys were starting to rip up their party napkins and make them into spitballs. That's when she got the idea for us to make the lists.

Ms. Babbitt told us we didn't have to turn them in, just take them home and think about them, so I didn't use my best handwriting.

Here's what I put:

I ♥ -

1. **My mother and father.**

2. **My big brother,** except when he calls me Beanhead, or eats all the sweet cereal before I get even one bowl, or turns the channel when I'm watching a program, or burps. Loud.

3. **My stuffed animal, Jingle Bell.** A moose. I love Jingle Bell because he listens when I talk and doesn't blab my secrets and when I say something dumb he doesn't call me Beanhead.

4. **My pearl necklace** that I got at a garage sale for fifty cents. It has four strands of huge pink pearls. I can't figure out why somebody wanted to sell it.

5. **My paper napkin collection from parties and restaurants.**

6. My star sweater. My star sweater
is a dark blue pullover sweater with white
stars knit all over it. Whenever I put on
my star sweater I feel like the night sky.
I can twirl across my bedroom like a
shooting star. I can wave my arms and
dance on my tiptoes like I'm twinkling.
I can spread out my arms and shine down
on all the earth.

A week after the valentine list, my star
sweater almost got taken away from me.

It happened the day Carol Ann taught me

a new way to color. She made me give her two Tootsie Roll Pops, cherry ones, before she'd show me. But it was worth it. She showed me how to peel the wrong end of the crayon and color with the side of it. If you press hard the color comes out dark at the edge, then lighter, like a shadow.

I peeled all my crayons except for my glow-in-the-dark ones that are so special I never even use them. Then I drew a shaded line with each one. While I did it I tried to memorize the names of all forty-eight colors. As I was brushing the crayon peelings under my bed, my mom came into my room to tell me that cousin Laura was coming over the next night. Mom asked me if it was all right for us to give Laura some of my old clothes.

"Sure," I answered. "Hey, Mom, look at this neat way to color I just learned."

The next night my Aunt Jean and Uncle Rich came to supper with their kids, Brett, Laura, and Evan. After supper we kids were at the dining room table setting up a Sorry game when I heard my mom in the kitchen telling Aunt Jean about my old clothes.

"There's a denim skirt that's too short and some sweatshirts she's outgrown and a cute sweater with stars on it that's way too tight," I heard Mom say.

I jumped up and raced through the dining room, through the living room, through the hall, up the stairs, into my room. I pulled the star sweater out of my drawer and got it stuffed behind my dresser just as Mom and Aunt Jean came into the room.

Then I went back to the Sorry game and told Laura I didn't think she looked good in blue. "Why don't you go up and tell my mom you don't want a blue sweater?" I said.

"I love blue," Laura answered.

"I'll give you one of my tiger posters if you go up and tell my mom you don't want the star sweater," I offered.

"Tigers are dumb," she said.

I wanted to tell her that I wished a tiger would eat her up, but instead I said, "Now periwinkle—that's your color." Periwinkle is a crayon color I memorized. I thought I could impress Laura with such a big word.

But it didn't work.

"No, blue is my color," she told me. "My mom said so. She said it matches my eyes." I told Laura her eyes were not blue. They were the color of a fish's skin.

"They are not! I'm telling what you said!" she screamed at me, and left the room.

My mother didn't find the sweater that night, but she told Laura she'd keep looking, because it was the perfect color to go with Laura's eyes.

At bedtime I rolled the star sweater into a ball and took it into bed with me and Jingle Bell. I told Jingle Bell about hiding the sweater. I only did it because I needed time to figure out how to explain to Mom about the sweater, so she wouldn't think I was being selfish. I wanted to tell her in just the right way so she wouldn't say, "You're being silly. That sweater is much too small and it's going to Laura and that's final, young lady."

I wanted Mom to understand that I didn't mind the sleeves coming just below my elbows and the neck being tight. I wanted to make her understand about feeling like the night sky.

In the morning I put the sweater back behind my dresser. I went down to the kitchen where Mom was sitting at the table in her old, ratty robe, the color of a pink carnation crayon.

When I came in she pulled me onto her lap.

"Do you like this robe of mine?" she asked.

"Well, it's kind of ratty-looking," I answered. "And that one place where you shut the front door on it and it ripped and you tried to patch it looks pretty sad."

Mom laughed. "I know it's been through

a lot. But your dad gave me this robe when I was in the hospital after I had you and I love it. I hope it holds together forever. Do you have anything you love like that?"

I looked down at my chewed-up nails. I brushed a piece of fuzz off my big toe. I picked at a scab on my knee. Finally I said, "I love my star sweater. I don't want to give it to Laura."

"Why didn't you tell me, Beany?"

"Because you might think I was being selfish and babyish."

"Did you really think I wouldn't care about how you felt or believe how much you wanted to keep the sweater?"

"Well, I didn't want to take a chance."

"My poor little worrywart," Mom said, and hugged me tight against her pink carnation robe.

"I have something to tell you," I said.

"I hid the sweater behind my dresser. Please don't be mad."

"I'm not mad."

"And I wished that a tiger would eat Laura," I added.

"Wishes don't make things happen. You know that, Beany."

"And I told Laura her eyes are the color of fish skin."

"Oh dear," my mother said. "That *is* a problem. What are you going to do about it?"

I thought about it for a minute. I decided I would draw Laura a picture of a beautiful fish with blue eyes and long lashes. I would color it in my new way that Carol Ann taught me. I would use my glow-in-the-dark crayons.

"I have an idea for the sweater," my mother said. We went upstairs. I pulled the sweater from its hiding place and gave it to Mom. She took the sweater in one hand and Jingle Bell in the other. She pulled the sweater over the moose's head and pulled his arms through the sleeves. Then I rolled up one blue, star-covered sleeve while she rolled up the other.

Jingle Bell looked like the night sky. I twirled him around. I danced across the room with him. I lifted him high and spread his arms out wide. Jingle Bell twinkled and sparkled and shined.

Beany

The Tooth

* * * *

One of my teeth came out right in the middle of lunch at school. It was a bottom tooth—two teeth to the left of the middle one—and it came out when I bit into an apple. I wrapped the tooth in a napkin and put it in my lunch box. During math I went to the nurse, Mrs. Facinelli, to show her my tooth and look at her wall chart of an eyeball.

On the bus ride home I showed the tooth to Carol Ann.

"How much do you get for a tooth?" she asked.

"Fifty cents," I said. "How much do you get?"

"I get seventy-five," she said, and grinned kind of a bragging grin. I hate it when she does that.

"No fair! How come you get so much more than me?"

"Do you floss?" Carol Ann asked.

"Sometimes. Well, only the day before I go to get my teeth cleaned."

"Do you leave a thank-you note under your pillow?"

"I didn't know you're supposed to. How come nobody ever tells me this stuff?"

"Okay, I'm going to help you out," Carol Ann said. "I'm going to tell you a list of rules I made up. Number one, soak your tooth in Polident false teeth cleaner for one hour till the dried up blood comes out of the hole in the middle of the tooth."

"I don't have any Polident," I said.

"I'll give you some of my grandfather's."

Carol Ann's grandfather lives with them. He has false teeth, but he doesn't wear them, except for church. Most of the time he keeps them in a peanut butter jar on the kitchen sink. I couldn't eat peanut butter for a week after I first saw Mr. Devlin's teeth soaking in that jar.

"Okay, what comes after the Polident?" I asked.

"Number two, brush the tooth with toothpaste. Number three, cover the tooth with clear nail polish to make it shine. Number four, leave the tooth under your pillow in a special box just for teeth."

"I don't have one!" I said when I heard number four. I started to bite my nails.

"Well, make one. Don't you know any-thing?" Carol Ann sighed and went on list-ing the rules. "Number five—and this is very important—leave a thank-you note under your pillow."

I asked Carol Ann if she would write down what she says in her thank-you notes.

She sighed again and said, "Oh, all right." I watched over her shoulder as she pulled a sheet of filler paper out of her backpack and wrote:

Dear Tooth Fairy,

Thank you for paying me for my tooth. I will not buy candy with the money. I floss every day.

From,
Carol Ann

PS: My sister Margo does not floss every day even if she says she does.

I stopped at Carol Ann's house on the way home from the bus stop. She gave me a plastic sandwich bag of Polident.

At supper I passed my tooth around the table so everyone could see it.

"It looks just like a little pearl," my mother said.

"It looks strong and healthy because you drink lots of milk," my father said.

"Gross. Get that thing out of my face," my brother said.

"I really think this tooth is worth seventy-five cents," I told everyone at the table.

That night, after I showed the tooth to Jingle Bell, I made a tooth box out of construction paper. Then I put all the things I would need on the bathroom sink. I put the box, a glass of water mixed with Polident, a toothpick and a safety pin for digging out the blood from the little hole in the middle

of the tooth, a toothbrush and a tube of tartar control toothpaste so the tooth wouldn't get any plaque, and a bottle of Flaming Fuschia nail polish. Carol Ann had said to use clear polish, but all I had was Flaming Fuschia that my grandmother bought me when I stayed at her house one weekend. My mother told me Flaming Fuschia is a teenage color, so I haven't used it yet.

I turned on the water and held my tooth under it to get off the bits of napkin and my brother's fingerprints, and then it happened: My tooth went down the drain.

For a few seconds I couldn't believe what had happened. Then I started yelling, "Emergency, emergency!" over and over again, until my parents and Philip came running up the stairs, asking if I was hurt or if I was sick. Philip wanted to call 911.

My dad turned off the water and took

apart all the pipes under the sink. But the tooth wasn't there. Philip said it was probably already miles away in the sewer, being eaten by a rat. My mother said, "Philip Jerome Sherwin-Hendricks, go to your room."

Then she sat on the toilet lid holding me in her lap and telling me everything would be all right.

That night my pillow was very lumpy. Underneath it I had put an empty tooth box, a note I wrote to the tooth fairy explaining about the tooth going down the drain, my thank-you note, a picture I drew of my mouth showing what spot the tooth came from, a picture of our bathroom sink after the pipes had been taken apart, and a poem I wrote.

Here are the pictures: ⟶

tooth out

under the sink

Here is the poem:

HOW I LOST MY TOOTH

I wiggled it and jiggled it

and squiggled it.

I couldn't get it out.

I pushed it and pulled it and turned it.

I couldn't get it out.

I couldn't get it out but my apple did.

I bit it and cried.

My tooth was inside,

All covered with blood.

Then it went down the sink

And that stinks.

The next morning at the bus stop Carol Ann asked me how much I got.

"My usual fifty cents," I said.

"Well, hand it over. My grandfather blew his top when he looked for his Polident and it was all gone. We have to buy him a new box."

The Talent Show

* * * *

Ms. Babbitt came to school one day wearing her smiley face earrings, the ones that mean something special is going to happen. Kelsey asked her why she was wearing them. But Ms. Babbitt said she wouldn't tell till the end of the day.

Right before dismissal Ms. Babbitt said, "Boys and girls, I have something special to announce. Two weeks from today this class is going to have a talent show. It'll be in the gym, and all the first, second, and third graders will come to see it. We won't have winners. We won't have prizes. It's just going to be for fun. You may perform anything you'd like—a poem, a song, a joke, a dance.

Are there any questions?"

Carol Ann asked, "Can we wear costumes?"

"You may wear costumes or not, whichever you prefer."

Steven asked, "Can we do stuff in groups?"

"You may perform alone or in groups."

Pam asked, "If we say a poem, do we have to rememberize it, or can we read it off a paper?"

"I think it would be much more effective if you memorized it."

Leo asked, "Can I have my dog in my act?"

"You may, but someone must bring the dog at the time of the show. It may not roam around our classroom all day distracting the class."

Wendy, who's shy and talks so quietly

you can hardly hear her, asked, "Do we have to do something?"

"No one has to be in the show, but I think those of you who choose to be a part of it will have lots of fun."

The dismissal bell rang and we all ran for the buses, talking about the talent show.

That night, Carol Ann called me on the phone. "Beany, I have the greatest idea for the talent show. You and I are going to recite a poem together. I wrote a poem that has lines for two people to say. It's about bees—a queen bee and a worker bee. It'll be the best act in the whole show. If they gave awards, this act would win first place. We'll practice every day after school. My mother will make the costumes. You'll be the worker bee and I'll be the queen bee."

"Why do you get to be the queen?" I asked.

"Because I have curly hair, silly. Don't you know anything?"

The next day Carol Ann gave me a copy of the poem. We practiced at her house after school. Carol Ann stretched out on big pillows to say her lines. I had to stand holding a mop and a pail. Carol Ann said those were props and they made us look our parts.

I didn't want to hold a pail and mop while Carol Ann lay on pillows, but I didn't complain because, number one, Carol Ann is very bossy and I'm a tiny bit scared of her and, number two, I didn't have any better ideas for an act.

The day after that we practiced at my house. Carol Ann wore a crown. I didn't.

On Saturday Carol Ann decided I should say my lines in a low, growly voice like a worker who is tired and she should say her lines soft and tinkly like a queen.

On Monday Carol Ann showed me

pictures she drew of the costumes. Carol Ann's had a gold ruffled ballerina skirt. Mine had a big black-and-yellow-striped T-shirt and black tights.

A week before the show Carol Ann said, "Let's talk about all the things that might go wrong."

"Let's not," I said.

Carol Ann ignored that and started to list them: "I'm worried you might forget your lines, or drop your mop, or get a run in your tights, or trip over your pail, or get the hiccups, or sneeze."

That's when I started to worry. I worried that I would spit when I talked. I worried that my antennae would fall down over my face. I worried that instead of saying, "I feed the queen and build the hive," I would say, "I feed the hive and build the queen."

Every night at supper I said my lines to

my family. Every night in bed I bit my nails thinking about doing the bee poem.

One night as I was repeating, "I feed the queen and build the hive," over and over during supper, my dad said, "Beany, relax. You're supposed to be enjoying this talent show."

"I know. Ms. Babbitt even said the show was for fun. But I'm not having any. I know I'll do something wrong and Carol Ann will be mad at me."

"Then why are you doing an act with her?" my brother asked.

"It just sort of happened. Besides, I don't have any better ideas."

"How about doing the cartwheels you just learned in gymnastics class?" my mother asked. "Your teacher said you do them really well."

"Carol Ann wouldn't like that. She's got everything all figured out for us."

That night as I lay in bed biting my nails, my dad tiptoed into my room.

"Are you awake?" he whispered.

"I can't sleep," I said. "I'm thinking about the bee poem."

"I want to show you something wonderful," Dad said. He swung me and Jingle Bell onto his back and carried us down the stairs and out the front door. There were two sleeping bags spread out on the driveway.

Jingle Bell and I lay on top of one of them and Dad lay on the other.

"Look at the sky," he said. "I don't think I've ever seen it so beautiful. I wanted to share it with you."

Dad was right. The sky looked like black ink. The stars looked like white polka dots.

"How many stars are there?" I asked my dad.

"Billions," he answered.

"I mean, what's the exact number?"

"That's a mystery."

"I'm going to count them," I decided. So I picked a spot to start at and tried to keep track of which stars I had counted and which ones were left. When I got to twenty-seven, I got mixed up and had to start over. This time I got to thirty-two before I got mixed up again. I started a third time.

Dad stopped me. "You know something, Beany? I don't think you should count the stars. There are some things in life that are just meant to be enjoyed."

"You mean like a dish of double chocolate ice cream with colored sprinkles and whipped cream on top?" I asked.

"Yes," he said, "and like a sausage, pepperoni, and onion pizza."

"And like kittens," I added.

"Right. And like Beethoven's Fifth Symphony."

"And like a starry, starry night, Daddy?"

"Yes, like a starry, starry night."

We looked up at the sky for a while. Then my dad asked, "Do you know what else should just be enjoyed?"

"What?"

"A talent show."

He reached over to my sleeping bag and

squeezed my hand. We lay there looking up at the stars for a long time. Not counting them. Just enjoying them.

The next day on the bus ride to school I took a deep breath and said to Carol Ann, "I don't want to do the bee poem. I want to do cartwheels across the gym floor."

"Why?" she asked.

"Because cartwheels are fun."

"What would you wear?"

"Shorts and a T-shirt."

"What kind of music would you have?"

"No music."

"How many cartwheels would you do?"

"As many as it takes."

"What if you fall?"

"I'll get up and keep going."

"What if you do a cartwheel into Kevin Gates?"

"Carol Ann, quit it," I said. "I'm doing

cartwheels no matter what you say." Then I gave her back the paper with my bee poem lines.

On Friday our class put on the best talent show in the whole world. For his talent, Boomer Fenton showed his birthmark in the shape of a dog's face. Kelsey played "Twinkle, Twinkle, Little Star" on her violin. Leo tried to get his dog to roll over, but the dog ran under Ms. Babbitt's chair and wouldn't come out for the rest of the show. Carol Ann and Wendy did the bee poem. Carol Ann's crown fell off right in the middle of it.

For my talent, I did cartwheels from one end of the gym to the other. It was fun.

The End

Susan Wojciechowski says that
the character of Beany came
into her head while she was in
bed with the flu. "Beany just
stayed there, and by the time
I was well, the stories were
written. The author of *The
Christmas Miracle of Jonathan
Toomey,* a picture book illustrated by P.J. Lynch, and *Patty
Dillman of Hot Dog Fame* and
other middle-grade novels,
Susan Wojciechowski lives
in York, Pennsylvania, with her
husband and three children.

Susanna Natti, the illustrator
of more than thirty books,
searched for a model for her
illustrations of Beany, finally
finding her in one of her
daughter's friends. "This child
is going to be a wonderful
actress someday," she says.
"I would read the scene from
the book and she would act
it out while I sketched." She
adds, "I love Beany; I think as
an illustrator you have to love
the characters."